JOLLY ROGER

Meet the pirates of Abdul the Skinhead in this swashbuckling riot of an adventure!

Colin McNaughton is a renowned poet and is recognized as one of Britain's leading children's authors and illustrators. He has produced over seventy books, including *Have You Seen Who's Just Moved in Next Door to Us?* (winner of the Kurt Maschler Award), *Captain Abdul's Pirate School* (winner of the British Design Production Award for Children's Books) and *Potty Poo-Poo Wee-Wee!* He is also the author of a popular series of humorous poetry that includes the collections *Wish You Were Here (And I Wasn't)* and *Making Friends with Frankenstein.*

Colin lives in London with his wife and two sons.

For the Conways
of Elvan Lodge

First published 1988 by Walker Books Ltd
87 Vauxhall Walk, London SE11 5HJ

This Sprinters edition published 2006

© 1988, 1992 Colin McNaughton

The right of Colin McNaughton to be identified as
author of this work has been asserted by him in accordance
with the Copyright, Designs and Patents Act 1988

This book has been typeset in Garamond

Printed and bound in Great Britain by J.H. Haynes & Co. Ltd

British Library Cataloguing in Publication Data:
a catalogue record for this book is available
from the British Library

ISBN-13: 978-1-4063-0617-0
ISBN-10: 1-4063-0617-7

www.walkerbooks.co.uk

COLIN McNAUGHTON
JOLLY ROGER
AND THE PIRATES OF CAPTAIN ABDUL

WALKER BOOKS

Contents

Characters

This is Roger, our hero.

This is Roger's mum.
Her name is Ernestine.

Part I
Roger's Lot

RATS! cursed Roger as he walked down to the shop in the port where he lived. "I'm fed up!"

"Mornin', Jolly Roger," said a passing youth. "What are you looking so grumpy about? Lost a shilling and found a penny, eh? Ha ha!"

Everyone called Roger "Jolly Roger" because he always looked so miserable.

The reason that Roger and his mum were so miserable was all because Roger's dad had disappeared when Roger was just a baby.

His dad had last been seen
talking to some pirates in an inn on
the coast of Africa. When his ship
returned, Roger's dad
was not on it.

Roger's mum
had never
smiled again.

Roger was turning
all this over in his
mind when he
reached the
grocery shop.
Taped to the
window was a poster.

JOYN THE PIRATES

- CABIN BOY REKWIRED
FOOL TRAYNIN GIVIN.
HOPERTOONHITY 4 TRAVIL

GUD PROMOSHUN PROSPEX

NO SOFTEES KNEED APPLY

SEE ABDUL the SKINHEAD
CAPTIN of the GOLDEN
BEHIND

his mark · Oooh-arrgh!

"That's it!" shouted Roger. "I'll join the pirates and run away to sea! Maybe I'll find my dad! And when I grow up and I'm all huge and hairy, I'll come home and say 'Ha!' to my mum. 'Take that, and that!'"

While Roger was pretending to slice up his mum like a salami, he failed to notice the pack

of horrible, hairy, dirty, smelly,
ugly, scary men creeping up on him.

Without so much as a "How do
you do" they stuffed young Roger
into a sack!

"'E'll do!" they shouted. "Just the
right size for a cabin boy! Let's get
'im back to the ship."

Part II
Kidnapped! Oooh-arrgh!

When Roger was tipped out of the sack, he found himself surrounded by pirates. All of them, he noted, had bits missing – fingers, eyes, ears, even legs!

"Belay below thar, me wee barnacle! Ha-har! Oooh-arrgh!" bellowed a great big hairy brute.

"Must be the captain," thought
Roger. "He's got more bits missing
than anybody else."

"Oooh-arrgh!" howled the captain again. "What be that 'orrible rotten smell, eh? Be that ye a-stinkin', landlubber? Pooh, it's disgustible!"

"I'm sorry," said Roger, "but can't you speak English?"

"HINGLISH!!!" stormed the captain. "Shiver me tonsils and avast me wooden leg! A-course I speaks the Hinglish, yer cheeky wee fish hook!"

(All pirates at this time in history spoke in this funny way. No one is sure why. Maybe it was because they were all extremely thick!)

"Well, you didn't have to press-gang me," said Roger. "I was just about to apply for the job anyway!"

"Oh," said the captain. "Well, what is that horrible pong a-waftin' across me poop deck?"

"It'll be the smell of soap, Cap'n!" said one of the pirates. "It's the wee lad there. He stinks of it!"

All the pirates cried:

"POOH!"

"YUK!" and

"PASS ME A CLOTHES-PEG BEFORE I'M SICK!"

"So," said the captain, "yer wants ter be a pirate, eh, soapy chops? What's yer name?"

Charming!

"It's Roger," said Roger.

"That's a useless name for a pirate," scoffed the captain. "If yer wants to be a real pirate, yer needs a nickname. Oooh-arrgh!"

"What sort of nickname?" asked Roger rather sulkily.

"Come on me hearties!" bellowed the captain. "Let's show him some real pirate nicknames! Oooh-arrgh! Sing him yer songs!"

And this is what the pirates sang:

"I suppose I do have a nickname," said Roger. "Because I look so miserable, folks call me Jolly Roger!"

"JOLLY ROGER!" roared the pirates. "That be perfeck! Oooh-arrgh! That's what we calls our flag – the Jolly Roger!"

"SHUT YER GOBS!" bawled Captain Abdul. "Let the lad speak. I wants to hear what makes him so grouchy."

"Well," said Roger, "it's my mum. She's the cleanest, tidiest, grumpiest person in the whole world. Every day I've got to make the beds, get washed, comb my hair, brush my teeth, do the dishes, bake the bread, scrub the floors, clean the pigsty, wash the cow, polish the goat, shampoo the chicken, whitewash the coal – on and on and on!"

What's a comb?

(Well it was almost true, thought Roger, crossing his fingers.)

"Poor wee scab!" growled the captain. "It ain't right for a lad to be brought up so clean!

"NO! Kids should be smelly an' 'orrible. It's the only chance they gets before they grow up into people! Unless they become pirates! Then they can be dirty, smelly, lazy an' 'orrible all their lives! Ya-har! Ain't that the truth, me hearties, eh? Oooh-arrgh!…

"What do you say, me lads? Should we go an' teach his mum a lesson? Should we go an' shiver her timbers?" "AYE!" roared the crew. "LET'S GO GET HER!"

The pirates swarmed into the
rowing boat, leaving only Roger
and the cook behind.

"Cookee!" yelled the captain.
"Give the lad some grub – he
needs buildin' up if he's goin'
ter be a pirate. Oooh-arrgh!"

Roger wanted to call out not to
hurt his mum, but it was too late.
The pirates were already speeding
towards the quay – the captain
water skiing behind.

Cookee gave Roger a huge plate of sausages and beans smothered in chocolate sauce and chopped bananas. It was delicious!

"Cookee," said Roger, "why didn't you have a song?"

"Oh, that's because I'm not a proper pirate. I do have a little song of my own but it's not a pirate song. You see, when I was press-ganged like you, they bopped me on the head and I lost my memory. That's what my song is about."

Is there anybody out there
  Who might know this little man?
Is there anybody out there
  Who can tell me who I am?

Can you tell me what my name is?
  Can you tell me where I'm from?
Was it Plymouth, York or London?
  Am I Harry, Dick or Tom?

Was I rich and was I famous,
  Was I poor, was I unknown?
Have I children and a wife somewhere,
  Or did I live alone?

Is there anybody out there
  Who might know this little man?
Is there someone, somewhere
  Who can tell me who on earth I am?

"Poor Cookee, that's the saddest song I've ever heard," said Roger, wiping a tear from his eye.

"Aye – well, that's the way the cookie crumbles," said Cookee with a chuckle. "Here, try this pirate suit on for size."

Roger cheered up at once when he saw himself in the mirror. "That's more like it!" he shouted. "Now I look like a real pirate!"

Part III
Roger to the Rescue

Roger and Cookee waited three
days for the pirates to return but
there was no sign of them. Not
even a postcard.

"We'd better go and see what's
happened," said Roger, who
was worried about his mum.
They hitched a lift from a
passing fisherman,
ran through the
port and crept
up to Roger's
little farm.

This is what they saw.

Roger's mum was in charge!
Smothered in swords
and pistols, she
had the pirates
working like
slaves!

Get to work!

Roger sneaked over to Khan the Really Nasty: "Psst, Khan! What happened?"

"Jolly Roger!" said Khan with a start. "We've been captured!"

"How?" said Roger. "There are eleven of you and only one of her!"

"When we got here," said Khan, "we shut her in the house and started havin' some fun: chuckin' things around an' breakin' things up. Well, then we found some rum an' we had a party! We got drunk as lords an' fell asleep. When we woke up we was chained hand an' foot. Prisoners! Since then it's been terrible! First she made us wash!

"Then she put us to work and every night she chains us up in the barn!"

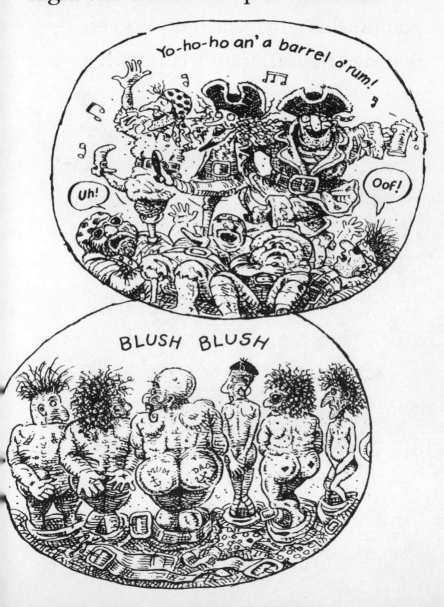

From across the farmyard Roger's
mum screamed, "KHAN! Haven't
you finished that washing-up yet,
you lazy barbarian?"

"Almost done, ma'am," replied Khan in a weedy little voice. "You'd better go!" he hissed to Roger. "We told her we'd press-ganged you an' she says unless we tell her where you are she's going to twist our ears off."

Roger crept back to Cookee and told him the bad news. "We must help them!" said Roger. "They'll never escape on their own."

"Right!" said Cookee. "But let's wait till it's dark."

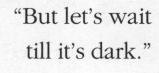

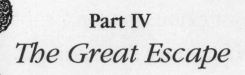

Part IV
The Great Escape

Just before dawn, Roger and
Cookee made
their move.
"Follow me,"
whispered
Roger.
"There are
some loose
boards round
the back of the
barn." Once inside, they crept up
to the slumbering pirates.

"Captain!" hissed Roger.

"WHAT? Curse yer! Who be that disturbin' me beauty sleep? Oooh-arrgh!"

"It's all right," said Cookee, "he's like this every morning when I take him his Rice Krispies soaked with rum."

Roger found the keys and set the pirates free.

"Let's go," he whispered, "but don't make a sound."

They were crossing the yard when:

"KABOOOOM!!!" roared a blunderbuss over their heads.

"Get back in that barn, you hooligans!" yelled Roger's mum.

"Arrgh!" howled the captain, stepping on a rake and blacking his good eye. "Be this the end of Abdul the Skinhead…?

"To die
so young,
oooh-arrgh,
in me prime!"

"Oh, come on,
you big baby!"
hissed Roger.

"That's no way to
talk to yer captain!"
whimpered Abdul.
"Men have walked
the plank for less!"

"Yes, well, we'll
discuss it later," said Roger.
"Meanwhile, let's get out of here!"

Through the streets the terrified pirates ran, Roger's mum hot on their heels.

What a sight! What a to-do! There hadn't been so much excitement since Sir Walter Raleigh opened the town's first fish and chip shop!

The pirates hurled themselves
into their rowing boat and furiously
set off, heaving and lurching across
the harbour.

"Come back here, you louts!"
yelled Roger's mum. "I'll teach you
to pinch my Roger!" And picking up
a wooden bucket...

she hurled it at the
escaping pirates.

It landed with
a mighty "CLONK!"
smack bang on
Cookee's hairy head, knocking him
senseless and sending him toppling
into the water.

"MAN OVERBOARD!" shouted
Roger. "Turn the boat around!"

"No fear!" barked Abdul.
"It's every man for
himself! Pull harder,
ye dogs, or there'll
be no cocoa in
bed tonight!
Oooh-arrgh!"

"Anyway," panted Riff-Raff Rafferty, "none of us can swim."

"CAN'T SWIM!" shouted Roger. And with these words our hero dived into the shark-infested waters (well, sardine-infested, actually).

At the same moment, Roger's mum dived from the quay. They reached Cookee just as he was going down for the third time.

Part V
Cookee tells all! EXCLUSIVE!

With the aid of a boat-hook
Cookee was lifted out of the
water and lain with a squelch
on the quay.

He slowly opened his
eyes, removed a sardine
from his mouth,
then spoke these
startling words:

"Ernestine! Is that
you? Don't you
recognize me?

"It's your long-lost husband, Henry!
That bang on the nut has given me
back me memory!"

Everyone gasped.

"DAD!" shouted Roger.

"HALLELUJAH!" cried Ernestine.

Then she did something Roger
had never seen in all his nine
years – she smiled.

Roger was shocked.

His mum's face was … well, pretty!

Meanwhile, well away from all that soppy nonsense, the pirates were heading in the general direction of somewhere a long way away from Roger's mum.

"I'd rather take me chances with a two-hundred-gun Spanish man-o-war than tackle that woman again!" roared the captain. "Next time ye press-gang a cabin boy make sure you take a look at his mum first!"

And so with a final "Oooh-arrgh!" we take our leave of the pirates of Abdul the Skinhead, and return to dry land.

Part VI
Celebration!

A party had started on the quay. There was much singing of sea shanties and much dancing of sailor-type jigs.

People laughed and people cried and a rollicking good time was had by all.

Roger's dad told of his adventures with the pirates, and Roger's mum told of the hard times they had been through.

Roger's dad had a shave and haircut. Without all that hair he was … well, quite handsome!

After a cracking party, Roger and
his mum and dad headed home.

"Come on," said Roger's mum.
"That farm won't run itself, you
know. There's work to be done!"

Roger and his dad burst out
laughing. "Aye-aye, Captain!" they
said. "Aye-aye!"

AUTHOR'S NOTE
You have probably noticed some awful
spelling in this book. Sorry, but that's the only
way I can show you how pirates spoke.
(Don't let your teacher see!)

Sprinters

Fun Sprinters for you to enjoy!

Captain Abdul's Pirate School	Colin McNaughton
Care of Henry	Anne Fine
Cool as a Cucumber	Michael Morpurgo
Cup Final Kid	Martin Waddell
Ernie and the Fishface Gang	Martin Waddell
Fearless Fitzroy	Kathy Henderson
Fighting Dragons	Colin West
The Finger-eater	Dick King-Smith
The Haunting of Pip Parker	Anne Fine
Impossible Parents	Brian Patten
Jolly Roger	Colin McNaughton
Lady Long-legs	Jan Mark
Molly and the Beanstalk	Pippa Goodhart
Nag Club	Anne Fine
No Tights for George!	June Crebbin
Patrick's Perfect Pet	Annalena McAfee
Posh Watson	Gillian Cross
The Snow Maze	Jan Mark
Star Striker Titch	Martin Waddell
Taking the Cat's Way Home	Jan Mark
Tarquin the Wonder Horse	June Crebbin
Tricky Nelly's Birthday Treat	Berlie Doherty
The Vampire Across the Way	Dyan Sheldon